Mistress Mary

Story by:
Lois Becker
Mark Stratton

Illustrated by:

Theresa Mazurek
Douglas McCarthy
Allyn Conley-Gorniak
Lorann Downer

Rivka
Fay Whitemountain
Su-Zan Lewis
Lisa Souza

This Book Belongs To:

Jennifer

Use this symbol to match book and cassette.

The nursery rhyme is called "Mistress Mary." And you'll get to visit Mary's garden and see how Hector helps Mary.

Mistress Mary, quite contrary,
How does your garden grow?
With silver bells and cockleshells,
And pretty maids all in a row.

"The Contrary Song"

Contrary people act in contrary ways
And give contrary answers to whatever you say;
If you nod your head "yes," they're sure to shake "no."
But if you say "no," they'll insist that it is so!
If you mention "day," they will tell you it's "night."
And if you say "dark," they will always say "bright!"

New and old, hot and cold,
Right and wrong, left and right.
Up and down, square and round,
High and low, black and white.

Yes, contrary people are contrary-wise:
If they see a cat sit, they'll tell you it flies!
They'll look at a dog and say it's a flea!
They'll show you an A and they'll say it's a Z!
They have to be different…no, that's not quite right!
They'd rather be opposite, that's their delight!

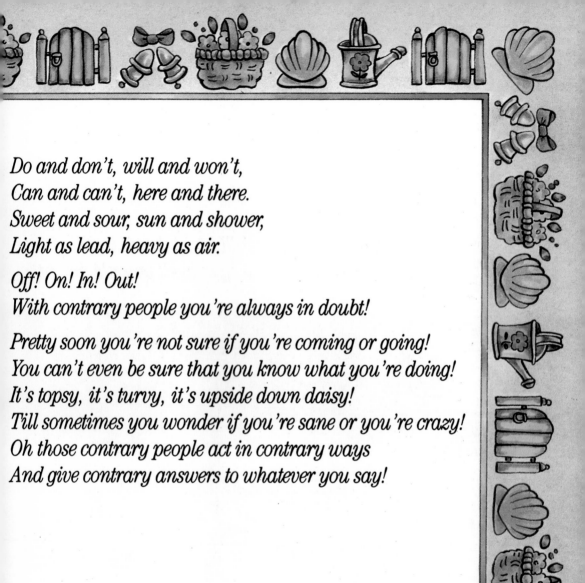

Do and don't, will and won't,
Can and can't, here and there.
Sweet and sour, sun and shower,
Light as lead, heavy as air.

Off! On! In! Out!
With contrary people you're always in doubt!

Pretty soon you're not sure if you're coming or going!
You can't even be sure that you know what you're doing!
It's topsy, it's turvy, it's upside down daisy!
Till sometimes you wonder if you're sane or you're crazy!
Oh those contrary people act in contrary ways
And give contrary answers to whatever you say!

Hector thought Mistress Mary needed
a friend. So he jumped into the pond
and paddled off to find her. On the way
he saw lots of different gardens and lots
of different gardeners...but no Mary.
Finally, Hector came to a high wall made
entirely of seashells.

So Hector hopped out of the pond, shook
himself off, and waddled over to ring the
silver bell by the gate.

A little shutter opened in the gate, and a girl with a sour face looked out.

It was Mistress Mary!

Hector asked Mistress Mary if he could see her garden. But Mary said that she never showed her garden to anyone. Then, just to be contrary, she decided to let Hector see it after all.

It was a very odd sort of garden, for there wasn't a bit of green in it. There were old silver bells hanging from leafless trees, dusty cockleshell paths and four statues standing side by side.

Those were the pretty maids all in a row.

All of a sudden, there was a loud noise and a tiny plant popped up from the earth!

When Mistress Mary saw it, she got really upset. She ran over, pulled it up, and threw it over the wall just as fast as she could!

But no sooner had she gotten rid of one plant than a dozen more popped up. And leaves began to sprout on all the trees!

Hector didn't know why Mistress Mary wanted to pull up the plants, but he helped her anyway.

Hector and Mistress Mary had such a good time pulling up the plants, that they decided to clean the whole garden together. First they polished the silver bells. Then they washed the cockleshell paths.

And finally they gave the statues a bubble bath!

A funny thing was happening to Mistress Mary. With each task, she became a little less contrary. First she started to smile, then she began to giggle, and finally she burst into laughter.

Then Hector told Mary that he was her friend.

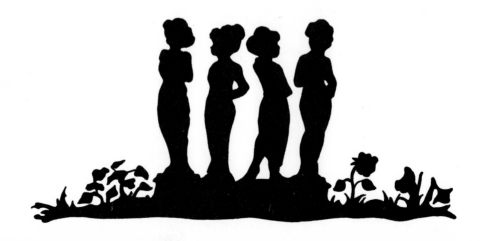

Mary felt happier than she had ever felt in her whole life. She felt so happy that she forgot to be contrary.

Mary even wanted to put plants in her garden. Hector thought he knew where they might find some plants. And sure enough, on the other side of the wall, all sorts of beautiful plants had taken root.

So Hector and Mistress Mary set about replanting the garden.

"I Like to Watch Things Grow!"

Gardens are made of growing things—
Planting, watering, hoeing things;
Grass and vines and shrubs and trees,
Butterflies and buzzing bees!

Chorus

I like to watch things grow!
I like to watch and know,
That by the love and care I give
I help the little plants to live!

I used to be contrary!
I thought all plants were weeds!
She pulled up every flower
And leaf from the tree!
But now…

Repeat Chorus

People are like gardens,
They need lots of care;
But all the love you give them
Comes back for you to share.
That's why…

I like to watch things grow!
I like to watch things grow!
I like to watch you grow, dear!
Plants and people!
Chicks and puppies!
Bunnies! Ducks!
And even guppies!
I like to watch things grow!
I like to watch things grow!

When they were finished, the garden looked beautiful.

And then a wonderful thing happened. The statues began to talk.

They had been afraid to say anything because Mistress Mary was so contrary!

Then it was time for Hector to say goodbye. Mistress Mary didn't want him to go. But Hector promised he'd be back to visit.

Mary gave Hector a cockleshell with a plant in it as a present.

Hector came back to tell me all about his special day.

Now that Mistress Mary isn't contrary anymore, people come from miles around to admire her garden.

And they love it because it's so beautiful.